NANA, NENEK & NINA

Liza Ferneyhough

Dial Books for Young Readers

this is nenek.

NEH-nek

the k is there, and not... like a ghost. start saying the k, but stop suddenly before any sound comes out.

brring

For my British-Malaysian-American family, especially my parents, who are Nenek & Granddad to Miles. Thanks, ta, and terima kasih!

Nina has two grandmothers who

Nina lives across the sea and

Nina is somewhere

live on opposite sides of the world.

Nenek lives across the other sea.

in between them.

If she misses them and wants to visit, there's a lot of figuring out to do.

Nina has to pack different things for Nana's house and Nenek's house,

but she always brings along something small to remind her of home.

To see Nana, Nina's family flies toward sunrise.

To see Nenek, they fly toward sunset instead.

Traveling tires Nina out.

Early the next morning, she wakes up

so she takes some time to rest.

and knows she is somewhere very different.

At Nana's,
it's usually damp and chilly.
Nina wriggles into some woolly things
and gets ready to go out.

cardigan

tights

mac
(raincoat)

umbrella

dungarees

pinny
(jumper)

wellies

(rainboots)

(overalls)

At Nenek's,
they start their day outside
before the sun gets too high in the sky.
Nina just has to slip on her selipar.

topi
(hat)

singlet
(tank top)

pelindung matahari
sun screen

dres
(sundress)

kaca mata hitam
(sunglasses)

seluar pendek
(shorts)

baju renang
(swimsuit)

selipar
(flip-flops)

Nana asks Nina for some help around the garden.

They make sure everyone

"Just a little," Nina tells the fish.
"A wee bit," agrees Nana.

Nenek needs some help around the halaman too.

has a good breakfast.

"Bok bok," Nina gathers the chickens.
"Ketuk-ketuk," they cluck.

Rain drops down as Nina hops from puddle to puddle.
When it gets too wet, Nana calls her inside for a cup of hot chocolate.

They play a game on Daddy's old noughts-and-crosses board.
Nina lines her crosses up, one, two, three.

Nina uses up all her outside voice in one loud shout.
When it gets too hot, Nenek calls her inside for a glass of iced Milo.

Her cousins get out Mama's old congkak set.
Nina clacks the marbles, satu, dua, tiga.

Sometimes Nina asks for a trip

ICE LOLLIES   FISH & CHIPS   candy floss

Nana and Nina poke the tips of
their toes in the water—brrr!
—and then look for fossils instead.

She digs a deep hole with Nana

to the seaside *pleeeeeease*.

Nenek and Nina go wading and
poke at tiny burrowing crabs.
Nina wants to burrow too.

and looks for its other end with Nenek.

Nana drives to the high street to chat with the greengrocer
and pop into some shops.
Her car rumbles over the cobblestones.
She buys . . .

tomato sauce

beans for breakfast

tea

jam tart

strawberry

cornish pasty

in the late afternoon, while Nina takes her nap.

Nenek rides to the market to bargain with the street vendors
and visit the food stalls.
Her motorbike putts into the village.
She buys . . .

soy sauce
KECAP

beans for dessert

teh

tat nenas
(pineapple tart)

mangosteen

karipap
(curry puff)

Peas keep rolling off Nina's fork.
She likes to stick them on with mashed potato.

at the dinner table to eat.

Nina blows on her rice until
it's cool enough to pick up with her right hand.

They've had a long day and

Nana washes her hair in the bathtub.

there's sand behind Nina's ears.

Nenek rinses her off next to the kolam.

Nana draws the curtains closed
as Nina scrambles up the ladder.

The moon she knows from home

Nenek latches the shutters
as Nina swishes under the mosquito netting.

glows far outside both windows.

Sometimes Nina misses Nana.

When she visits, it's nice not to miss them.

Nana gives her a kiss.

They both love Nina

Sometimes she misses Nenek.

She'll miss home instead for a little while.

Nenek sniffs her cheek.

and she loves them too.

Dial Books for Young Readers · An imprint of Penguin Random House LLC, New York

First published in the United States of America by Dial Books for Young Readers, an imprint of Penguin Random House LLC, 2022

Copyright © 2022 by Liza Ferneyhough

Dial & colophon are registered trademarks of Penguin Random House LLC. · Visit us online at penguinrandomhouse.com.

Library of Congress Cataloging-in-Publication Data is available.

Manufactured in China · ISBN 9780593353943 · TOPL · 10 9 8 7 6 5 4 3 2 1

Design by Cerise Steel · Text set in Halewyn

The illustrations for this book were painted on tea-stained paper, using watercolors, many tiny brushes, and a crow quill dip pen. They were edited digitally.